9/18

9700-0046

THE COLLECTED WORKS OF
BILLY THE KID

Left Handed Poems

by MICHAEL ONDAATJE

Anansi

I send you a picture of Billy made with the Perry shutter as quick as it can be worked — Pyro and soda developer. I am making daily experiments now and find I am able to take passing horses at a lively trot square across the line of fire — bits of snow in the air — spokes well defined — some blur on top of wheel but sharp in the main — men walking are no trick — I will send you proofs sometime. I shall show you what can be done from the saddle without ground glass or tripod — please notice when you get the specimens that they were made with the lens wide open and many of the best exposed when my horse was in motion.

These are the killed.

(By me) —
Morton, Baker, early friends of mine.
Joe Bernstein. 3 Indians.
A blacksmith when I was twelve, with a knife.
5 Indians in self defence (behind a very safe rock).
One man who bit me during a robbery.
Brady, Hindman, Beckwith, Joe Clark,
Deputy Jim Carlyle, Deputy Sheriff J. W. Bell.
And Bob Ollinger. A rabid cat
birds during practice,

These are the killed.

(By them) —
Charlie, Tom O'Folliard
Angela D's split arm,
                              and Pat Garrett
sliced off my head.
Blood a necklace on me all my life.

Christmas at Fort Sumner, 1880. There were five of us together then. Wilson, Dave Rudabaugh, Charlie Bowdre, Tom O'Folliard, and me. In November we celebrated my 21st birthday, mixing red dirt and alcohol — a public breathing throughout the night. The next day we were told that Pat Garrett had been made sheriff and had accepted it. We were bad for progress in New Mexico and cattle politicians like Chisum wanted the bad name out. They made Garrett sheriff and he sent me a letter saying move out or I will get you Billy. The government sent a Mr. Azariah F. Wild to help him out. Between November and December I killed Jim Carlyle over some mixup, he being a friend.

Tom O'Folliard decided to go east then, said he would meet up with us in Sumner for Christmas. Goodbye goodbye. A few days before Christmas we were told that Garrett was in Sumner waiting for us all. Christmas night. Garrett, Mason, Wild, with four or five others. Tom O'Folliard rides into town, leaning his rifle between the horse's ears. He would shoot from the waist now which, with a rifle, was pretty good, and he was always accurate.

Garrett had been waiting for us, playing poker with the others, guns on the floor beside them. Told that Tom was riding in alone, he went straight to the window and shot O'Folliard's horse dead. Tom collapsed with the horse still holding the gun and blew out Garrett's window. Garrett already halfway downstairs. Mr. Wild shot at Tom from the other side of the street, rather unnecessarily shooting the horse again. If Tom had used stirrups and didnt swing his legs so much he would probably have been locked under the animal. O'Folliard moved soon. When Garrett had got to ground level, only the horse was there in the open street, good and dead. He couldnt shout to ask Wild where O'Folliard was or he would've got busted. Wild started to yell to tell Garrett though and Tom killed him at once. Garrett fired at O'Folliard's flash and took his shoulder off. Tom O'Folliard screaming out onto the quiet Fort Sumner street, Christmas night, walking over to Garrett, no shoulder left, his jaws tilting up and down like mad bladders going. Too mad to even aim at Garrett. Son of a bitch son of a bitch, as Garrett took clear aim and blew him out.

Garrett picked him up, the head broken in two, took him back upstairs into the hotel room. Mason stretched out a blanket neat in the corner. Garrett placed Tom O'Folliard down, broke open Tom's rifle, took the remaining shells and placed them by him. They had to wait till morning now. They continued their poker game till six a.m. Then remembered they hadnt done anything about Wild. So the four of them went out, brought Wild into the room. At eight in the morning Garrett buried Tom O'Folliard. He had known him quite well. Then he went to the train station, put Azariah F. Wild on ice and sent him back to Washington.

In Boot Hill there are over 400 graves. It takes
the space of 7 acres. There is an elaborate gate
but the path keeps to no main route for it tangles
like branches of a tree among the gravestones.

300 of the dead in Boot Hill died violently
200 by guns, over 50 by knives
some were pushed under trains — a popular
and overlooked form of murder in the west.
Some from brain haemorrhages resulting from bar fights
at least 10 killed in barbed wire.

In Boot Hill there are only two graves that belong to women
and they are the only known suicides in that graveyard

The others, I know, did not see the wounds appearing in the sky, in the air. Sometimes a normal forehead in front of me leaked brain gasses. Once a nose clogged right before me, a lock of skin formed over the nostrils, and the shocked face had to start breathing through mouth, but then the mustache bound itself in the lower teeth and he began to gasp loud the hah! hah! going strong — churned onto the floor, collapsed out, seeming in the end to be breathing out of his eye — tiny needle jets of air reaching into the throat. I told no one. If Angela D. had been with me then, not even her; not Sallie, John, Charlie, or Pat. In the end the only thing that never changed, never became deformed, were animals.

MMMMMMMM mm thinking
moving across the world on horses
body split at the edge of their necks
neck sweat eating at my jeans
moving across the world on horses
so if I had a newsman's brain I'd say
well some morals are physical
must be clear and open
like diagram of watch or star
one must eliminate much
that is one turns when the bullet leaves you
walk off see none of the thrashing
the very eyes welling up like bad drains
believing then the moral of newspapers or gun
where bodies are mindless as paper flowers you dont feed
or give to drink
that is why I can watch the stomach of clocks
shift their wheels and pins into each other
and emerge living, for hours

When I caught Charlie Bowdre dying
tossed 3 feet by bang bullets giggling
at me face tossed in a gaggle
he pissing into his trouser legs in pain
face changing like fast sunshine o my god
o my god billy I'm pissing watch
your hands
                while the eyes grew all over his body

              Jesus I never knew that did you
              the nerves shot out
              the liver running around there
              like a headless hen jerking
              brown all over the yard
              seen that too at my aunt's
              never eaten hen since then

Blurred a waist high river
foam against the horse
riding naked clothes and boots
and pistol in the air

Crossed a crooked river
loving in my head
ambled dry on stubble
shot a crooked bird

Held it in my fingers
the eyes were small and far
it yelled out like a trumpet
destroyed it of its fear

After shooting Gregory
this is what happened

I'd shot him well and careful
made it explode under his heart
so it wouldnt last long and
was about to walk away
when this chicken paddles out to him
and as he was falling hops on his neck
digs the beak into his throat
straightens legs and heaves
a red and blue vein out

Meanwhile he fell
and the chicken walked away

still tugging at the vein
till it was 12 yards long
as if it held that body like a kite
Gregory's last words being

get away from me yer stupid chicken

Tilts back to fall
black hair swivelling off her
shattering the pillow
Billy she says
the tall gawky body spitting electric
off the sheets to my arm
leans her whole body out
so breasts are thinner
stomach is a hollow
where the bright bush jumps
this is the first time
bite into her side leave
a string of teeth marks
she hooks in two and covers me
my hand locked
her body nearly breaking off my fingers
pivoting like machines in final speed

later my hands cracked in love juice
fingers paralysed by it arthritic
these beautiful fingers I couldnt move
faster than a crippled witch now

The barn I stayed in for a week then was at the edge of a farm and had been deserted it seemed for several years, though built of stone and good wood. The cold dark grey of the place made my eyes become used to soft light and I burned out my fever there. It was twenty yards long, about ten yards wide. Above me was another similar sized room but the floors were unsafe for me to walk on. However I heard birds and the odd animal scrape their feet, the rotten wood magnifying the sound so they entered my dreams and nightmares.

But it was the colour and light of the place that made me stay there, not my fever. It became a calm week. It was the colour and the light. The colour a grey with remnants of brown — for instance those rust brown pipes and metal objects that before had held bridles or pails, that slid to machine uses; the thirty or so grey cans in one corner of the room, their ellipses, from where I sat, setting up patterns in the dark.

When I had arrived I opened two windows and a door and the sun poured blocks and angles in, lighting up the floor's skin of feathers and dust and old grain. The windows looked out onto fields and plants grew at the door, me killing them gradually with my urine. Wind came in wet and brought in birds who flew to the other end of the room to get their aim to fly out again. An old tap hung from the roof, the same colour as the walls, so once I knocked myself out on it.

For that week then I made a bed of the table there and lay out my fever, whatever it was. I began to block my mind of all thought. Just sensed the room and learnt what my body could do, what it could survive, what colours it liked best, what songs I sang best. There were animals who did not move out and accepted me as a larger breed. I ate the old grain with them, drank from a constant puddle about twenty yards away from the barn. I saw no human and heard no human voice, learned to squat the best way when shitting, used leaves for wiping, never ate flesh or touched another animal's flesh, never entered his boundary. We were all aware and allowed each other. The fly who sat on my arm, after his inquiry, just went away, ate his disease and kept it in him. When I walked I avoided the cobwebs who had places to grow to, who had stories to finish. The flies caught in those acrobat nets were the only murder I saw.

And in the barn next to us there was another granary, separated by just a thick wood door. In it a hundred or so rats, thick rats, eating and eating the foot deep pile of grain abandoned now and fermenting so that at the end of my week, after a heavy rain storm burst the power in those seeds and brought drunkenness into the minds of those rats, they abandoned the sanity of eating the food before them and turned on each other and grotesque and awkwardly because of their size they went for each other's eyes and ribs so the yellow stomachs slid out and they came through that door and killed a chipmunk — about ten of them onto that one striped thing and the ten eating each other before they realised the chipmunk was long gone so that I, sitting on the open window with its thick sill where they couldnt reach me, filled my gun and fired again and again into their slow wheel across the room at each boommm, and reloaded and fired again and again till I went through the whole bag of bullet supplies — the noise breaking out the seal of silence in my ears, the smoke sucked out of the window as it emerged from my fist and the long twenty yard space between me and them empty but for the floating bullet lonely as an emissary across and between the wooden posts that never returned, so the rats continued to wheel and stop in the silences and eat each other, some even the bullet. Till my hand was black and the gun was hot and no other animal of any kind remained in that room but for the boy in the blue shirt sitting there coughing at the dust, rubbing the sweat of his upper lip with his left forearm.

PAULITA MAXWELL: THE PHOTOGRAPH

In 1880 a travelling photographer came through Fort Sumner.
Billy posed standing in the street near old Beaver Smith's saloon.
The picture makes him rough and uncouth.

The expression of his face was really boyish and pleasant.
He may have worn such clothes as appear in the picture out on
the range, but in Sumner he was careful of his personal appear-
ance and dressed neatly and in good taste. I never liked the
picture. I don't think it does Billy justice.

Not a story about me through their eyes then. Find the beginning, the slight silver key to unlock it, to dig it out. Here then is a maze to begin, be in.

Two years ago Charlie Bowdre and I criss-crossed the Canadian border. Ten miles north of it ten miles south. Our horses stepped from country to country, across low rivers, through different colours of tree green. The two of us, our criss-cross like a whip in slow motion, the ridge of action rising and falling, getting narrower in radius till it ended and we drifted down to Mexico and old heat. That there is nothing of depth, of significant accuracy, of wealth in the image, I know. It is there for a beginning.

She leans against the door, holds
her left hand at the elbow
with her right, looks at the bed

on my sheets — oranges
peeled half peeled
bright as hidden coins against the pillow

she walks slow to the window
lifts the sackcloth
and jams it horizontal on a nail
so the bent oblong of sun
hoists itself across the room
framing the bed the white flesh
of my arm

she is crossing the sun
sits on her leg here
sweeping off the peels

traces the thin bones on me
turns toppling slow back to the pillow
Bonney Bonney

I am very still
I take in all the angles of the room

January at Tivan Arroyo, called Stinking Springs more often. With me, Charlie, Wilson, Dave Rudabaugh. Snow. Charlie took my hat and went out to get wood and feed the horses. The shot burnt the clothes on his stomach off and lifted him right back into the room. Snow on Charlie's left boot. He had taken one step out. In one hand had been an axe, in the other a pail. No guns.

Get up Charlie, get up, go and get one. No Billy. I'm tired, please. Jesus watch your hands Billy. Get up Charlie. I prop him to the door, put his gun in his hand. Take off, good luck Charlie.

He stood there weaving, not moving. Then began to walk in a perfect, incredible straight line out of the door towards Pat and the others at the ridge of the arroyo about twenty yards away. He couldnt even lift his gun. Moving sideways at times but always always in a straight line. Dead on Garrett. Shoot him Charlie. They were watching him only, not moving. Over his shoulder I aimed at Pat, fired, and hit his shoulder braid. Hadnt touched him. Charlie hunched. Get up Charlie kill him kill him. Charlie got up poking the gun barrel in snow. Went straight towards Garrett. The others had ducked down, but not Garrett who just stood there and I didnt shoot again. Charlie he knew was already dead now, had to go somewhere, do something, to get his mind off the pain. Charlie went straight, now closer to them his hands covered the mess in his trousers. Shoot him Charlie shoot him. The blood trail he left straight as a knife cut. Getting there getting there. Charlie getting to the arroyo, pitching into Garrett's arms, slobbering his stomach on Garrett's gun belt. Hello Charlie, said Pat quietly.

Snow outside. Wilson, Dave Rudabaugh and me. No windows, the door open so we could see. Four horses outside.

Jim Payne's grandfather told him that he met Frank James of the James Brothers once.

It was in a Los Angeles movie theatre. After the amnesty he was given, Frank had many jobs. When Jim's grandfather met him, he was the doorman at the Fresco Theatre.

GET YOUR TICKET TORN UP BY FRANK JAMES the poster said, and people came for that rather than the film. Frank would say, 'Thanks for coming, go on in'.

Jim's grandfather asked him if he would like to come over and have a beer after the film, but Frank James said 'No, but thank you' and tore up the next ticket. He was by then an alcoholic.

Miss Angela Dickinson of Tucson
tall legs like a dancer
set the 80's style
by shaving them hairless
keeps saying
I'm too tall for you Billy
but we walk around a bit
buy a bottle and she stands
showing me her thighs
look Billy look at this
she folded on the sheet
tapping away at her knees
leans back waving feet at me
catching me like a butterfly
in the shaved legs in her Tucson room

A river you could get lost in
and the sun a flashy hawk
on the edge of it

a mile away you see the white path
of an animal moving through water

you can turn a hundred yard circle
and the horse bends dribbles his face
you step off and lie in it propping your head.

till dusk and cold and the horse shift you
and you look up and moon a frozen bird's eye

His stomach was warm
remembered this when I put my hand into
a pot of luke warm tea to wash it out
dragging out the stomach to get the bullet
he wanted to see when taking tea
with Sallie Chisum in Paris Texas

With Sallie Chisum in Paris Texas
he wanted to see when taking tea
dragging out the stomach to get the bullet
a pot of luke warm tea to wash it out
remembered this when I put my hand into
his stomach was warm

Pat Garrett, ideal assassin. Public figure, the mind of a doctor, his hands hairy, scarred, burned by rope, on his wrist there was a purple stain there all his life. Ideal assassin for his mind was unwarped. Had the ability to kill someone on the street walk back and finish a joke. One who had decided what was right and forgot all morals. He was genial to everyone even his enemies. He genuinely enjoyed people, some who were odd, the dopes, the thieves. Most dangerous for them, he understood them, what motivated their laughter and anger, what they liked to think about, how he had to act for them to like him. An academic murderer — only his vivacious humour and diverse interests made him the best kind of company. He would listen to people like Rudabaugh and giggle at their escapades. His language was atrocious in public, yet when alone he never swore.

At the age of 15 he taught himself French and never told anyone about it and never spoke to anyone in French for the next 40 years. He didnt even read French books.

Between the ages of 15 and 18 little was heard of Garrett. In Juan Para he bought himself a hotel room for two years with money he had saved and organised a schedule to learn how to drink. In the first three months he forced himself to disintegrate his mind. He would vomit everywhere. In a year he could drink two bottles a day and not vomit. He began to dream for the first time in his life. He would wake up in the mornings, his sheets soaked in urine 40% alcohol. He became frightened of flowers because they grew so slowly that he couldnt tell what they planned to do. His mind learned to be superior because of the excessive mistakes of those around him. Flowers watched him.

After two years he could drink anything, mix anything together and stay awake and react just as effectively as when sober. But he was now addicted, locked in his own game. His money was running out. He had planned the drunk to last only two years, now it continued into new months over which he had no control. He stole and sold himself to survive. One day he was robbing the house of Juanita Martinez, was discovered by her, and collapsed in her living room. In about six months she had un-iced his addiction. They married and two weeks later she died of a consumption she had hidden from him.

What happened in Garrett's mind no one knows. He did not drink, was never seen. A month after Juanita Garrett's death he arrived in Sumner.

PAULITA MAXWELL:
>I remember the first day Pat Garrett ever
>set foot in Fort Sumner. I was a small girl
>with dresses at my shoe-tops and when he
>came to our house and asked for a job, I
>stood behind my brother Pete and stared
>at him in open eyed wonder; he had the
>longest legs I'd ever seen and he looked so
>comical and had such a droll way of talking
>that after he was gone, Pete and I had a
>good laugh about him.

His mind was clear, his body able to drink, his feelings, unlike those who usually work their own way out of hell, not cynical about another's incapacity to get out of problems and difficulties. He did ten years of ranching, cow puching, being a buffalo hunter. He married Apolinaria Guitterrez and had five sons. He had come to Sumner then, mind full of French he never used, everything equipped to be that rare thing — a sane assassin sane assassin sane assassin sane assassin sane assassin sane

(Miss Sallie Chisum, later Mrs. Roberts, was living in Roswell in 1924, a sweet faced, kindly old lady of a thousand memories of frontier days.)

ON HER HOUSE

The house was full of people all the time
the ranch was a little world in itself
I couldn't have been lonesome if I had tried

Every man worth knowing in the Southwest,
and many not worth knowing, were guests
one time or another.
What they were made no difference in their welcome.
Sometimes a man would ride up in a hurry
eat a meal in a hurry and depart in a hurry

Billy the Kid would come in often
and sometimes stayed for a week or two.
I remember how frightened I was the first time he came.

Forty miles ahead of us, in almost a straight line, is the house. Angela D and I on horses moving towards it, me bringing her there. Even now, this far away, I can imagine them moving among the rooms. It is nine in the morning. They are leaning back in their chairs after their slow late Saturday breakfast. John with the heels of his brown boots on the edge of the table in the space he cleared of his plate and cup and cutlery, the cup in his hands in his lap. The table with four plates — two large two small. The remnants of bacon fat and eggs on the larger ones, the black crumbs of toast butter and marmalade (Californian) on the others. One cup in a saucer, one saucer that belonged to the cup that is in John Chisum's hands now. Across the table on the other side is Sallie, in probably her long brown and yellow dress, the ribbon down her front to the waist with pale blue buttons, a frill on either side of her neck along her shoulders. By now she would have moved the spare chair so she too could put her feet up, barefoot as always, her toes crinkling at the wind that comes from the verandah door. Her right arm would be leaning against the table and now and then she'll scrape the bottom of her cup against the saucer and drink some of the coffee, put it down and return the fingers of her right hand to bury them in the warm of her hair. They do not talk much, Sallie and John Chisum, but from here I can imagine the dialogue of noise — the scraping cup, the tilting chair, the cough, the suction as an arm lifts off a table breaking the lock that was formed by air and the wet of the surface.

On other days they would go their own ways. Chisum would be up earlier than dawn and gone before Sallie even woke and rolled over in bed, her face blind as a bird in the dark. It was only later, when the sun eventually reached the bed and slid over her eyes, that she slowly leaned up to find her body, clothesless, had got cold and pulling the sheet from the strong tuck fold at the foot of the bed brings it to her, wraps it around her while she sits in bed, the fists of her feet against her thighs trying to discover which was colder — the flesh at her feet or the flesh at her thighs, hugging the sheet to her tight until it would be a skin. Pretending to lock her arms over it as if a tight dress, warming her breasts with her hands through the material.

Once last year seeing her wrapped I said, Sallie, know what a mad man's skin is? And I showed her, filling the automatic indoor bath with warm water and lifting her and dropping her slow into the bath with the sheet around her and then heaving her out and saying that's what it is, that white thing round you. Try now to dig yourself out of it. Placed her in the bed and watched her try to escape it then.

On weekdays anyway, she'd sit like that on the bed, the sheet tight around her top and brought down to her belly, her legs having to keep themselves warm. Listening for noises around the house, the silence really, knowing John had gone, just leaving a list of things he wanted her to do. She would get up and after a breakfast that she would eat wandering around the house slowly, she would begin the work. Keeping the books, dusting his reading books, filling the lamps in the afternoon — they being emptied in the early morning by John to avoid fire danger when the sun took over the house and scorched it at noon, or dropping sideways in the early afternon sent rays horizontal through the doors and windows. No I forgot, she had stopped that now. She left the paraffin in the lamps; instead had had John build shutters for every door and window, every hole in the wall. So that at eleven in the morning all she did was close and lock them all until the house was silent and dark blue with sunless quiet. For four hours. Eleven till three. A time when, if inside, as I was often, your footsteps sounded like clangs over the floors, echoes shuddering across the rooms. And Sallie like a ghost across the room moving in white dresses, her hair knotted as always at the neck and continuing down until it splayed and withered like eternal smoke half way between the shoulder blades and the base of cobble spine.

Yes. In white long dresses in the dark house, the large bones somehow taking on the quietness of the house. Yes I remember. After burning my legs in the fire and I came to their house, it must have been my second visit and Sallie had begun using the shutters at eleven. And they brought the bed out of the extra bedroom and propped me up at one end of the vast living room of their bungalow. And I sat there for three days not moving an inch, like some dead tree witnessing the tides or the sun and the moon taking over from each other as the house in front of me changed colour — the night, the early morning yellow, the gradual move to dark blue at 11 o clock, the new white 4 o clock sun let in, later the gradual growing dark again.

For three days, my head delirious so much I thought I was going blind twice a day, recognizing no one, certainly not the Chisums, for I had been brought out cold and dropped on their porch by someone who had gone on without waiting even for water for himself. And Sallie I suppose taking the tent sheet off my legs each morning once the shutters closed. No. Again. Sallie approaching from the far end of the room like some ghost. I didn't know who it was, a tray of things in her right hand, a lamp in the other carrying them. Me screaming stop stop STOP THERE you're going to *fall* on me! My picture now sliding so she with her tray and her lamp jerked up to the ceiling and floated down calm again and jerked to the ceiling and floated down calm again and continued forward crushing me against the wall only I didnt feel anything yet. And Sallie I suppose taking the sheet off my legs and putting on the fan so they became cold and I started to feel them again. Then starting to rub and pour calamine like ice only it felt like the tongue of a very large animal my god I remember each swab felt like the skin and flesh had been moved off completely leaving only raw bone riddled with loose nerves being blown about and banging against each other from just her slow breath.

In the long 20 yard living-dining room I remember the closing of shutters, with each one the sudden blacking out of clarity in a section of the room, leaving fewer arcs of sun each time digging into the floor. Sallie starting from one end and disappearing down to the far end leaving black behind her as she walked into the remaining light, making it all a cold darkness. Then in other rooms not seen by me. Then appearing vast in the thick blue in her long white dress, her hands in the pockets strolling in the quiet, because of her tallness the hips moving first, me at the far end all in black.

Her shoes off, so silent, she moves a hand straying over the covers off John's books, till she comes and sits near me and puts her feet up shoeless and I reach to touch them and the base of them is hard like some semi-shelled animal but only at the base, the rest of her foot being soft, oiled almost so smooth, the thin blue veins wrapping themselves around the inside ankle bone and moving like paths into the toes, the brown tanned feet of Sallie Chisum resting on my chest, my hands rubbing them, pushing my hands against them like a carpenter shaving wood to find new clear pulp smelling wood beneath. My own legs black with scars. And down the room, the parrot begins to talk to itself in the dark, thinking it is night.

She had lived in that house fourteen years, and every year she demanded of John that she be given a pet of some strange exotic breed. Not that she did not have enough animals. She had collected several wild and broken animals that, in a way, had become exotic by their breaking. Their roof would have collapsed from the number of birds who might have lived there if the desert hadnt killed three quarters of those that tried to cross it. Still every animal that came within a certain radius of that house was given a welcome, the tame, the half born, the wild, the wounded.

I remember the first night there. John took me to see the animals. About 20 yards away from the house, he had built vast cages, all in a row. They had a tough net roof over them for the day time when they were let out but tended to stay within the shade of their cages anyway. That night John took me along and we stepped off the porch, left the last pool of light, down the steps into the dark. We walked together smoking his long narrow cigars, with each suck the nose and his mustache lighting up. We came to the low brooding whirr of noise, night sleep of animals. They were stunning things in the dark. Just shapes that shifted. You could peer into a cage and see nothing till a rattle of claws hit the grid an inch from your face and their churning feathers seemed to hiss, and a yellow pearl of an eye cracked with veins glowed through the criss crossed fence.

One of the cages had a huge owl. It was vast. All I could see were its eyes — at least 8″ apart. The next morning however, it turned out to be two owls, both blind in one eye. In those dark cages the birds, there must have been 20 of them, made a steady hum all through the night — a noise you heard only if you were within five yards of them. Walking back to the house it was again sheer silence from where we had come, only now we knew they were moving and sensing the air and our departure. We knew they continued like that all night while we slept.

Half way back to the house, the building we moved towards seemed to be stuffed with something yellow and wet. The night, the dark air, made it all mad. That fifteen yards away there were bright birds in cages and here John Chisum and me walked, strange bodies. Around us total blackness, nothing out there but a desert for seventy miles or more, and to the left, a few yards away, a house stuffed with yellow wet light where within the frame of a window we saw a woman move carrying fire in a glass funnel and container towards the window, towards the edge of the dark where we stood.

(To come) to where eyes will
move in head like a rat
-mad since locked in a biscuit tin all day
stampeding mad as a mad rats legs
bang it went was hot
under my eye
was hot small bang did it
almost a pop
I didnt hear till I was red
had a rat fyt in my head
sad billys body glancing out
body going as sweating white horses go
reeling off me wet
scuffing down my arms
wet horse white
screaming wet sweat round the house
sad billys out
floating barracuda in the brain

With the Bowdres

She is boiling us black coffee
leaning her side against the warm stove
taps her nails against the mug
Charlie talking on about things
and with a bit the edge of my eye
I sense the thin white body of my friend's wife

Strange that how I feel people
not close to me
as if their dress were against my shoulder
and as they bend down
the strange smell of their breath
moving across my face
or my eyes
magnifying the bones across a room
shifting in a wrist

Getting more difficult
things all over crawling
in the way
gotta think through
the wave of ants on him
millions a moving vest up his neck
over his head down his back
leaving a bright skull white smirking
to drop to ankles
ribs blossoming out like springs
the meat from his eyes

Last night was dreamed into a bartender
with an axe I drove into glasses of gin lifted up to be tasted

I have seen pictures of great stars,
drawings which show them straining to the centre
that would explode their white
if temperature and the speed they moved at
shifted one degree.

Or in the East have seen
the dark grey yards where trains are fitted
and the clean speed of machines
that make machines, their
red golden pouring which when cooled
mists out to rust or grey.

The beautiful machines pivoting on themselves
sealing and fusing to others
and men throwing levers like coins at them.
And there is there the same stress as with stars,
the one altered move that will make them maniac.

MISTUH...PATRICK...GARRETT ! ! !

Mescalaro territory is a flat region, no rivers, no trees, no grass.
In August the winds begin and at that time everybody who can
moves away. If you stayed, you couldnt see the sun for weeks
because, if opened, your eyes would be speckled and frosted
with sand. Dust and sand stick to anything wet as your eyeball,
or a small dribble from your nostril, a flesh wound, even sweat
on your shirt. A beard or mustache weighs three times as much
after you are caught in the storms. Your ears are so blocked that
you cannot hear for a good while afterwards, which is just as
well for all there is is the long constant screech and scream of
wind carrying anything it can lift.

I had been caught in the Mescalero that August for two days.
Blindfolding the horse I veered it east when the storm let down,
came to stony land and tumbleweed. Tumbleweed wont survive
in the Mescalero for it is blasted to pieces in minutes. But here,
tumbleweed moved like tires out of nowhere; you could be
knocked off your horse by them. In another half day I got to the
Chisum ranch. Had been there once a few years earlier and
had liked them very much. It was, anyway, the only place you
could have superb meals which became even better by your
realisation that there was nothing near them for almost a 100
miles. I arrived at their house mind blasted, and spent those
strange three hours while the Chisums rushed around me,
giving me drinks, gesturing towards the bath they had poured —
all in total silence for I heard nothing, only the wind I
remembered from 24 hours back — before my ears had been
gradually sprayed and locked. I put my head under water and
weaved about, the hot water stinging even more my red face.
Drunk on water, I staggered from the tub and passed out
on the bed.

Sallie came in when I was waking and threw me a towel. Can
you hear now? I nodded. Her voice like piercing explosions.
Yes, but softly, I said. She nodded. We got visitors, she said.
Do you know him? William Bonney? He's brought his girl-
friend that he plans to marry. My mind awake then. I'd of course

heard of him. But leaning back to think of it, I fell asleep. Sallie must have covered me up properly with a sheet because I woke up a long while later and was warm. I could hear the boy Bonney arguing with John.

I joined them just as they were finishing dinner. Bonney seemed relaxed and dressed very well, his left heel resting on his right knee. He ate corn, drank coffee, used a fork and knife alternately — always with his right hand. The three days we were together and at other times in our lives when we saw each other, he never used his left hand for anything except of course to shoot. He wouldn't even pick up a mug of coffee. I saw the hand, it was virgin white. Later when we talked about it, I explained about how a hand or muscle unused for much work would atrophy, grow small. He said he did fingers exercises subconsciously, on the average 12 hours a day. And it was true. From then on I noticed his left hand churning within itself, each finger circling alternately like a train wheel. Curling into balls, pouring like waves across a tablecloth. It was the most hypnotising beautiful thing I ever saw.

He jumped up, and introduced himself informally to me, not waiting for Chisum to, and pointed out Angie. She was a good 6″ taller than him, a very big woman, not fat, but big bones. She moved like some fluid competent animal.

Bonney was that weekend, and always was, charming. He must, I thought, have seduced Angie by his imagination which was usually pointless and never in control. I had expected him to be the taciturn pale wretch — the image of the sallow punk that was usually attached to him by others. The rather cruel smile, when seen close, turned out to be intricate and witty. You could never tell how he meant a phrase, whether he was serious or joking. From his eyes you could tell nothing at all. In general he had a quick, quiet humour. His only affectation was his outfit of black clothes speckled with silver buttons and silver belt lock. Also his long black hair was pulled back and tied in a knot of leather.

It was impossible to study the relationship he had with the large tall Angie. After dinner they sat in their chairs. He would usually be hooked in ridiculous positions, feet locked in the chair's arms, or lying on the floor with his feet up. He could never remain in one position more than five minutes. Angie alternately never moved violently like Billy. Only now and then she shifted that thick body, tucked her legs under those vast thighs that spread like bags of wheat, perfectly proportioned.

After an evening of considerable drinking we all retreated to our rooms. And the next morning, Billy and Angie who had been planning to leave, decided to stay. I was glad as I didnt understand either of them and wanted to see how they understood each other. At breakfast a strange thing happened that explained some things.

Sallie had had a cat named Ferns who was very old and had somehow got pains in its shoulders during the last two days. I looked at it after breakfast and saw it had been bitten by a snake. It was in fact poisoned and could not live. It already had gone half blind. John decided then to kill it and lifted the half paralysed body to take it outside. However, once out, the cat made a frantic leap, knowing what was going to happen, fell, and pulled itself by two feet under the floor boards of the house. The whole of the Chisum house was built in such a way that the house stood on a base which was 9" off the ground. The cat was heard shifting underneath those floors and then there was silence. We all looked under the boards from the side of the house, seeing into the dark, but we couldnt see Ferns and couldnt crawl under to get him. After a good hour, from the odd thrashing, we knew the cat was still alive and in pain. It would I theorized probably live for a day and then die. We sat around on the verandah for a while and then Billy said, do you want me to kill it. Sallie without asking how said yes.

He stood up and took off his boots and socks, went to his room, returned, he had washed his hands. He asked us to go into the living room and sit still. Then he changed his mind and asked us to go out of the house and onto the verandah and keep still and quiet, not to talk. He began to walk over the kitchen floor, the living room area, almost bent in two, his face about a foot from the pine floorboards. He had the gun out now. And for about half an hour he walked around like this, sniffing away it seemed to me. Twice he stopped in the same place but continued on. He went all over the house. Finally he came back to a spot near the

44

sofa in the living room. We could see him through the window, all of us. Billy bent quietly onto his knees and sniffed carefully at the two square feet of floor. He listened for a while, then sniffed again. Then he fired twice into the floorboards. Jumped up and walked out to us. He's dead now Sallie, dont worry.

Our faces must have been interesting to see then. John and Sallie were thankful, almost proud of him. I had a look I suppose of incredible admiration for him too. But when I looked at Angie, leaning against the rail of the verandah, her face was terrified. Simply terrified.

Down the street was a dog. Some mut spaniel, black and white. One dog, Garrett and two friends, stud looking, came down the street to the house, to me.

Again.

Down the street was a dog. Some mut spaniel, black and white. One dog, Garrett and two friends came down the street to the house, to me.

Garrett takes off his hat and leaves it outside the door. The others laugh. Garrett smiles, pokes his gun towards the door. The others melt and surround.
All this I would have seen if I was on the roof looking.

You know hunters
are the gentlest
anywhere in the world

they halt caterpillars
from path dangers
lift a drowning moth from a bowl
remarkable in peace

in the same way assassins
come to chaos neutral

Snow outside. Wilson, Dave Rudabaugh and me. No windows, the door open so we could see. Four horses outside. Garrett aimed and shot to sever the horse reigns. He did that for 3 of them so they got away and 3 of us couldnt escape. He tried for 5 minutes to get the reigns on the last horse but kept missing. So he shot the horse. We came out. No guns.

One morning woke up
Charlie was cooking
and we ate not talking
but sniffing wind
wind so fine
it was like drinking ether

we sat hands round knees
heads leaned back taking lover wind
in us sniffing and sniffing
getting high on the way
it crashed into our nostrils

This is Tom O'Folliard's story, the time I met him, eating red dirt to keep the pain away, off his body, out there like a melting shape in the sun. Sitting, his legs dangling like tails off the wall. Out of his skull.

What made me notice him was his neck. Whenever he breathed the neck and cheek filled out vast as if holding a bag of trapped air. I introduced myself. Later he gave me red dirt. Said want to hear a story and he told me. I was thinking of a photograph someone had taken of me, the only one I had then. I was standing on a wall, at my feet there was this bucket and in the bucket was a pump and I was pumping water out over the wall. Only now, with the red dirt, water started dripping out of the photo. This is his story.

At fifteen he took a job with an outfit shooting wild horses. They were given a quarter a head for each one dead. These horses grazed wild, ate up good grass. The desert then had no towns every 50 miles. He sucked the clear milk out of a chopped cactus, drank piss at times. Once, blind thirsty, O'Folliard who was then 17 killed the horse he sat on and covered himself in the only liquid he could find. Blood caked on his hair, arms, shoulders, everywhere. Two days later he stumbled into a camp.

Then half a year ago he had his big accident. He was alone on the Carrizoza, north of here; the gun blew up on him. He didnt remember anything after he saw horses moving in single file and he put the gun to his shoulder. Pulling the trigger the gun blew to pieces. He was out about two days. When he woke up, he did because he was vomiting. His face was out to here. From that moment, his horse gone, he lived for four days in the desert without food or water. Because he had passed out and eaten nothing he survived, at least a doctor told him that. Finding water finally, he drank and it poured out of his ear. He felt sleepy all the time. Every two hours he stopped walking and fell asleep placing his boots into an arrow in the direction he was going. Then he would get up, put boots on and move on. He said he would have cut off his left hand with a knife to have something to eat, but he realised he had lost too much blood already.

He killed lizards when he got onto rock desert. Then a couple of days later the shrubs started appearing with him following them, still sleeping every two hours. First village he came to was Mexican. José Chavez y Chavez, blacksmith. The last thing O'Folliard noticed was Chavez sandbagging him in the stomach. O'Folliard going out cold. When he woke José had him in a bed, his arms trapped down.

Chavez had knocked out Tom as he had gone to throw himself in water which would have got rid of his thirst but killed him too. Chavez gave it to him drop by drop. A week later he let Tom have his first complete glass of water. Tom would have killed Chavez for water during that week. When he finally got to a doctor he found all the muscles on the left side of his face had collapsed. When he breathed, he couldnt control where the air went and it took new channels according to its fancy and formed thin balloons down the side of his cheek and neck. These fresh passages of air ricocheted pain across his face every time he breathed. The left side of his face looked as though it had melted by getting close to fire. So he chewed red dirt constantly, his pockets were full of it. But his mind was still sharp, the pain took all the drug. The rest of him was flawless, perfect. He was better than me with rifles. His feet danced with energy. On a horse he did tricks all the time, somersaulting, lying back. He was riddled with energy. He walked, both arms crooked over a rifle at the elbows. Legs always swinging extra.

MISS SALLIE CHISUM : ON BILLY

I was sitting in the living room
when word was brought he had arrived.
I felt in a panic. I pictured him
in all the evil ugliness
of a bloodthirsty ogre.
I half expected he would slit my throat
if he didnt like my looks.

I heard John saying with a wave of his hand,
Sallie, this is my friend, Billy the Kid.
A good looking, clear-eyed boy stood there
with his hat in his hand, smiling at me.

I stretched out my hand automatically to him,
and he grasped it in a hand as small as my own

Crouching in the 5 minute dark
can smell him smell that mule sweat
that stink need a shotgun
for a searchlight to his corner

Garrett? I aint love-worn
torn aint blue I'm waiting
smelling you across the room
to kill you Garrett going
to take you from the knee up
leave me   my dark   AMATEUR!

A motive? some reasoning we can give to explain all this violence. Was there a source for all this? yup —

"Hill leaped from his horse and, sticking a rifle to the back of Tunstall's head blew out his brains. Half drunk with whisky and mad with the taste of blood, the savages turned the murder of the defenceless man into an orgy. Pantillon Gallegos, a Bonito Cañon Mexican, hammered in his head with a jagged rock. They killed Tunstall's horse, stretched Tunstall's body beside the dead animal, face to the sky, arms folded across his breast, feet together. Under the man's head they placed his hat and under the horse's head his coat carefully folded by way of pillows. So murdered man and dead horse suggested they had crawled into bed and gone to sleep together. This was their devil's mockery, their joke — ghastly, meaningless. Then they rode back to Lincoln, roaring drunken songs along the way.

"Lucky for Billy the Kid and Brewer that they had gone hunting wild turkeys, else they would have shared Tunstall's fate. From a distant hillside they witnessed the murder."

To be near flowers in the rain
all that pollen stink buds
bloated split
leaves their juices
bursting the white drop of spend
out into the air at you
the smell of things dying flamboyant
smell stuffing up your nose
and up like wet cotton in the brain
can hardly breathe nothing
nothing thick sugar death

In Mexico the flowers
like brain the blood drained out
packed with all the liquor perfume
sweat like lilac urine smell
getting to me from across a room

if you cut the stalk
your face near it
you feel the puff of air escape
the flower gets small smells sane
deteriorates in a hand

When Charlie Bowdre married Manuela, we carried them
on our shoulders, us on horses. Took them to the Shea
Hotel, 8 rooms. Jack Shea at the desk said
Charlie — everythings on the house, we'll give you the
Bridal.
No no, says Charlie, dont bother, I'll hang onto her ears
until I get used to it.

HAWHAWHAW

White walls neon on the eye
1880   November 23   my birthday

catching flies with my left hand
bringing the fist to my ear
hearing the scream grey buzz
as their legs cramp their
heads with no air
so eyes split and release

open fingers
the air and sun hit them like pollen
sun flood drying them red
catching flies
angry weather in my head, too

I remember this midnight at John Chisum's. Sallie was telling me about Henry. They had had it imported from England by ship, then train, then Sallie had met the train and brought it the last seventy miles in a coach. Strangest looking thing she said. It could hardly walk up a stair at first because it was so heavy and long. Its tail, which was dark brown with an amber ridge all down the middle of its length, stood up like a plant, so when he moved up and down hills the first thing you saw was this tail. In the house, John's clock banged away in the kitchen, the noise and whir reeling out onto us on the porch. John and Sallie, the mut Henry, and me. I had come in that morning.

They call it a bassett says Sallie, and they used to breed them in France for all those fat noblemen whose hounds were too fast for them when they went hunting. So they got the worst and slowest of every batch and bred them with the worst and slowest of every other batch and kept doing this until they got the slowest kind of hound they could think of. Looks pretty messy to me, I said. John scratched his groin awkwardly but politely — I mean not many would have noticed if they hadnt been on the lookout, expecting it as it were. **John began a story.**

When I was in New Orleans during the war I met this character who had dogs. I met him because I was a singer then, and he liked to sing, so we used to sing together quite a lot. He seemed a pretty sane guy to me. I mean, he didnt twitch or nothing like that. Well, a month or two after I left New Orleans, I got a note from another friend who sang with us once in a while, and he said Livingstone, who was the first singer, had been eaten by his dogs. It was a postcard and it didnt say anymore. When I was in New Orleans again, 2 or 3 years later I found out.

Livingstone had been mad apparently. Had been for a couple of years, and, while he couldnt fight in the war — he had a limp from a carriage accident — he hung around the soldiers like me. There was a rumour though that the reason he was not accepted was because no one that knew him would trust him with a gun. He had almost killed his mother with a twelve bore, fortunately only shooting an ugly vase to pieces and also her foot. (Her surgeon's bills were over $40 for he took nearly three hours getting all the buckshot out of her thighs because she wouldnt let anyone go any further than her knees, not even a professional doctor.) After that, Livingstone stayed away from guns, was embarrassed by it all I suppose, and besides the episode was a joke all over town.

Some time later he bought a spaniel, one of the American kind. A month later he bought another. He said he was going to start breeding dogs, and his mother, pleased at even a quirk of an ambition, encouraged him. But she didnt realize what he had been really doing until after his death and even then the vet had to explain it to her once more. Livingstone, and this was at the same time as he sang with me in the evenings, had decided to breed a race of mad dogs. He did this by inbreeding. His mother gave him money to start the business and he bought this wooden walled farm, put a vast fence around an area of 50 square feet, and keeping only the two original dogs he had bought, literally copulated them into madness. At least not them but their pups, who were bred and re-bred with their brothers and sisters and mothers and uncles and nephews. Every combination until their bones grew arched and tangled, ears longer than their feet, their tempers became either slothful or venomous and their jaws were black rather than red. You realize no one knew about this. It

60

went on for two or three years before the accident. When people asked him how the dogs were coming along, he said fine; it was all a secret system and he didnt want anyone looking in. He said he liked to get a piece of work finished before he showed it to people. Then it was a surprise and they would get the total effect. It was like breeding roses.

You are supposed to be able to tell how inbred a dog is by the width of their pupils and Livingstone knew this, for again he picked the two most far gone dogs and bred them one step further into madness. In three years he had over 40 dogs. The earlier ones he just let loose, they were too sane. The rest, when the vet found them, were grotesque things — who hardly moved except to eat or fornicate. They lay, the dogs, when they found his body, listless as sandbags propped against the 14 foot fence Livingstone had built. Their eyes bulged like marbles; some were blind, their eyes had split. Livingstone had found that the less he fed them the more they fornicated, if only to keep their mind off the hunger. These originally beautiful dogs were gawky and terrifying to that New Orleans vet when he found them. He couldnt even recognize that they had been spaniels or were intended to be. They didnt snarl, just hissed through the teeth — gaps left in them for they were falling out. Livingstone had often given them just alcohol to drink.

His mother continued to give him money for his business, which still of course hadnt turned a penny. He had never sold a dog and lived alone. He came into town on Thursdays for food and on Thursday evenings when I was stationed in New Orleans he sang with me. We usually drank a lot after the bouts of singing. And again, even when drunk he never showed any sign of madness or quirkiness. As if he left all his madness, all his perverse logic, behind that fence on his farm and was washed pure by the time he came to town every Thursday. Many he had known when younger said how much more stable he had become, and that now they probably would accept him in the army. He told me he had a small farm he ran, never mentioning dogs. Then usually about three in the morning or around then he went back home to the house next to those 40 mad dogs, clinically and scientifically breeding the worst with the worst, those heaps of bone and hair and sexual organs and bulging eyes and minds which were chaotic half out of hunger out of liquor out of their minds being pressed out of shape by new freakish bones that grew into their skulls. These spaniels, if you could call them that now, were mostly brown.

When they found Livingstone there was almost nothing left of him. Even his watch had been eaten by one of the dogs who coughed it up in the presence of the vet. There were the bones of course, and his left wrist — the hand that held the whip when he was in the pen — was left untouched in the middle of the area. But there was not much else. The dust all over the yard was reddish and his clothes, not much left of those, scattered round.

The dogs too were blood hungry. Though this scene was discovered, they reckoned, two days after the event occurred, some of the dogs had been similarly eaten. The vet went into the house, got Livingstone's shot gun, the same one that had spread bullets into his mother's leg, couldnt find any bullets, went into town, bought bullets, didnt say a word in town except got the sherriff with him and rode back. And they shot all the dogs left, refusing to go into the pen, but poking the gun through the planks in the fence and blowing off the thirty heads that remained alive whenever they came into range or into the arc that the gun could turn to reach them. Then they went in, dug a pit with a couple of Livingstone's shovels, and buried everything. 40 dogs and their disintegrated owner.

The clock inside whirred for a half second and then clunked 1 o clock. Sallie got up and walked down the steps of the porch. Henry could deal with the steps now, went down with her and they walked into the edge of the dark empty desert. John rocked on in his chair. I was watching Sallie. She bent down, put her hands under Henry's ears and scratched his neck where she knew he liked it. She bent down further to his ear, the left one, the one away from us, and said, very quietly, I dont think John heard it it was so quiet, Aint that a nasty story Henry, aint it? Aint it nasty.

Up with the curtain
down with your pants
William Bonney
is going to dance

Hlo folks —'d liketa sing my song about the lady Miss A D
you all know her — her mind the only one in town high on
the pox

Miss Angela D has a mouth like a bee
she eats and off all your honey
her teeth leave a sting on your very best thing
and its best when she gets the best money

           Miss Angela Dickinson
           blurred in the dark
           her teeth are a tunnel
           her eyes need a boat

           Her mouth is an outlaw
           she swallow your breath
           a thigh it can drown you
           or break off your neck

           Her throat is a kitchen
           red food and old heat
           her ears are a harp
           you tongue till it hurt

           Her toes take your ribs
           her fingers your mind
           her turns a gorilla
           to swallow you blind

           (thankin yew

Angela — hand shot open
water blood on my shoulder
crying quiet
O Bonney you bastard Bonney
kill him Bonney kill him

this from Angela
she saying this when their bullet for me
split her wrist so flesh burst out

Watching me do it.
Took knife and opened the skin
more, tugged it back
on the other side of her arm
to pick the bullets out
3 of them
like those rolled pellet tongues of pigeons

look at it, I'm looking into your arm
nothing confused in there
look how clear
Yes Billy, clear

So we are sitting slowly going drunk here on the porch. Usually it was three of us. Now five, our bodies on the chairs out here blocking out sections of the dark night. And the burn from the kerosene lamp throwing ochre across our clothes and faces. John in the silent rocking chair bending forward and back, one leg tucked under him, with each tilt his shirt smothering the light and spiralling shadows along the floor. The rest of us are quieter. Garrett sits on the sofa with Sallie the quietest of us all. He doesnt talk much I've noticed and mostly listens. Sallie her legs out resting on the chair at the ankles, the long skirt falling like a curtain off her legs and touching the floor. The cat shifts in her lap. And just to my left, her leg dangling off the rail she sits on, Angela D, the long leg about a foot to my left swaying, the heel tapping the wooden rail.

The thing here is to explain the difference of this evening. That in fact the Chisum verandah is crowded. It could of course hold a hundred more, but that John and Sallie and I have been used to other distances, that we have talked slowly through nights expecting the long silences and we have taken our time thinking the replies. That one was used to the space of black that hung like cotton just off the porch lights' spill. At 1 or 2 then Sallie would get up and bring me the cat and leave to make coffee and get ready for bed. And come back with the three cups and changed into her nightgown, always yellow or white with fabulous bows at her shoulders and the front of her neck. And then hunch up the gown over her folded legs so we joked at her looking like a pelican or some fat bird with vast stomach and short legs. But she didnt move from that, said her legs against herself kept herself warm for the wind had begun now, a slight flapping against the house. And it is now one and Sallie gets up and the cat stays on the sofa in the warm pool of material where she was. And Angela stretches and says bed I guess and I say no we are having coffee now and she leans back and later Sallie brings mugs in on a tray this time. And we all laugh a little cos Garrett has fallen asleep. Nobody noticed it in the semi dark. He hasnt moved an inch. Just the eyes closed. But the coffee tonight doesnt do much for the drink. That is, we are all pretty loaded here and in fact we go back to the whisky. And my throat now feels nothing as the drinks go down. I wonder how Angie can balance on the rail; as I do, she slips down near me and tho I cant see Sallie's eyes I think she must be watching us.

We sit here drinking on, after the coffee. Garrett here but asleep, Sallie, John, and the two of us. My eyes are burning from the pain of change and the whisky and I cant see very well, John's rocker is going slow but his checkered shirt leaves just a red arc daze like some blurred picture. I remember, when they took the picture of me there was a white block down the fountain road where somebody had come out of a building and got off the porch onto his horse and ridden away while I was waiting standing still for the acid in the camera to dry firm.

So, bed, says John and we say yes and sit for a bit longer, then Sallie wakes Garrett and we all get up and go to our rooms. And Angie I find is high as hell and stumbling hanging onto my shoulder. In the room we have been given the same bed I was given when alone. Angie says she'll have to sleep on top of me or me on top of her. And I say I'm too drunk for a balancing act Angie.O fooo she says and buttons open my shirt and her hands are like warm gloves on my back, soft till she uses her nails to scratch me towards her and I come and start giggling, wait the bathroom hold it. Yes, she says laughing. Quiet Sallie's in the next room, got ears like anything.

On the can I have to sit cos I know I cant pee straight. Before I finish she comes in and straddles me and drops her long hair into my open shirt as we slip our tongues into each others mouths. Her skirt over both of us and the can. Billy come on. mmm I say yes, get up first. No. Shit Angie. No. And slowly and carefully she lifts her legs higher and hangs them on tight to my shoulders like clothespins. Come on Angie I'm drunk 'm not a trapeze artist. Yes you are. No. And slowly I lift her up pressing her to me. The smell of her sex strong now daubing my chest and shirt where she rubs it. Youre too heavy for this I think, and we move careful to the floor, she leaning back like timber, lifts her legs to take clothes off and I grab the skirt and pull it over her head. Let me out Billy. Out Billy.Quiet she's next door. No! I know you Billy you! Youre fucking her. No Angie, no, I say, honest Angie you got too much, and enter her like a whale with a hat on, my drowning woman my lady who drowns, and take my hat off.

Waking in the white rooms of Texas after a bad night must be like heaven I think now. About 9 o clock and the room looks huge like the sun came in and pushed out the walls, now the sun — as if reflected off the bushes outside — hitting and swirling on the white walls and the white sheets on the bed as I can see when I put my head up.

I'm sure everyone in the house threw up last night. All except Garrett anyway. The whisky and coffee and whisky again did in our communal stomach and the bathroom last night was like a confession box. At one point Angela was in the can and Sallie and I stood in the hall, leaning against the wall, eyes half closed, she in a nightgown of white with silver flowers on it and a bow of grey trailing down to her stomach. The hall also grey as nobody wants the light on for our eyes are shifting like old half dried blood under their lids and Sallie's even put her hair over her face for more shade. And in my blur she looks lovely there, her body against the cold stone wall, leaning there, her arms folded, the wrists snuggled into her elbows and her gown down to her white feet scratching at each other. Me in a towel, having now to sit cos I keep slipping down the wall.

Hurry up Angela, Sallie hits the door. More noises in there like an engine starting up. I cant wait, I said, I'll go outside. No reply. And I move through the dark house hitting stools with my feet and hanging onto chairs on my way, cant see a goddam. Realize walls are there just before I hit them and the dog comes out of a corner and along with me licking my bare feet.

Outside with only a towel on and the wind is lifting the sand and lashing me around. I select a spot and start throwing up, the wind carrying it like a yellow ribbon a good foot to my right. The acid burning my gums and tongue on the way out. Stop. Put my fingers into the mushrooms of my throat and up it comes again and flies out like a pack of miniature canaries. A flock. A covey of them, like I'm some magician or something. This is doing nothing for my image is it. Here I am ¾s naked in a towel vomiting 10 yards from the house, to my left a fucking big desert where nothing is except wind picking up sand and dust and the smell off dead animals a hundred miles away and aiming it at me and my body.

And this bloody dog goes over and sniffs it and then methodically begins to eat, preparing no doubt his appetite for tomorrow morning, while now, it puts the machinery in me that organizes my throwing up to sleep, as if I hadnt drunk a thing in a year. I kick the dog away but it comes back to the meal. I cant yell cos my mouth is dry. I try and then the muscles heave deep down and up it comes like a daisy chain whipping out as it gets free into the slip stream of the wind and collapses on the ground right in front of the dog who is having the time of his life. The end. I leave the dog and move back into the now warm of the house, sand on my feet and collapse into my bed. And Angela's there and Sallie wasnt in the hall so I guess she's in there or back in bed. And just as I drop off I hear John getting up and staggering in the dark.

So it was a bad night. But this morning the room is white and silvery shadows roll across the ceiling. All is clean except our mouths and I move to the basin and rinse out last night's throat and pee down the drain and struggle back to bed, and Angela D is golden and cool beside me the sheet over her stomach like a skirt and her arm out straight over the edge of the bed like a peninsula rich with veins and cooler than the rest of her for it has been in the path of the window's wind all night.

She is so brown and lovely, the sun rim blending into lighter colours at her neck and wrists. The edge of the pillow in her mouth, her hip a mountain further down the bed. Beautiful ladies in white rooms in the morning. How do I wake her? All the awkwardness of last night with the Chisums gone, like my head is empty, scoured open by acid. My head and body open to every new wind direction, every nerve new move and smell. I look up. On the nail above the bed the black holster and gun is coiled like a snake, glinting also in the early morning white.

The street of the slow moving animals
while the sun drops in perfect verticals
no wider than boots
The dogs sleep their dreams off
they are everywhere
so that horses on the crowded weekend
will step back and snap a leg

/ while I've been going on
the blood from my wrist
has travelled to my heart
and my fingers touch
this soft blue paper notebook
control a pencil that shifts up and sideways
mapping my thinking going its own way
like light wet glasses drifting on polished wood.

The acute nerves spark
on the periphery of our bodies
while the block trunk of us
blunders as if we were
those sun drugged horses

I am here with the range for everything
corpuscle muscle hair
hands that need the rub of metal
those senses that
that want to crash things with an axe
that listen to deep buried veins in our palms
those who move in dreams over your women night
near you, every paw, the invisible hooves
the mind's invisible blackout   the intricate never
the body's waiting rut.

The eyes bright scales
(watch) bullet claws coming
at me like women fingers
part my hair slow
go in slow in slow,
leaving skin in a puff
behind and the slow
as if fire pours out
red grey brain the hair slow
startled by it all pour
Miss Angela D her eyes like a boat
on fire her throat is a kitchen
warm on my face heaving
my head mouth out
she swallows your breath
like warm tar pour
the man in the bright tin armour star
blurred in the dark
saying stop jeesus jesus jesus JESUS

This nightmare by this 7 foot high doorway
waiting for friends to come
mine or theirs
I am 4 feet inside the room
in the brown cold dark
the doorway's slide of sun
three inches from my shoes
I am on the edge of the cold dark
watching the white landscape in its frame
a world that's so precise
every nail and cobweb
has magnified itself to my presence

Waiting
nothing breaks my vision
but flies in their black path
like inverted stars,
or the shock sweep of a bird
that's grown too hot
and moves into the cool for an hour

If I hold up my finger
I blot out the horizon
if I hold up my thumb
I'd ignore a man who comes
on a three mile trip to here
The dog near me breathes out
his lungs make a pattern of sound
when he shakes
his ears go off like whips
he is outside the door
mind clean, the heat
floating his brain in fantasy

I am here on the edge of sun
that would ignite me
looking out into pitch white
sky and grass overdeveloped to meaninglessness
waiting for enemies' friends or mine

There is nothing in my hands
though every move I would make
getting up slowly walking
on the periphery of black
to where weapons are
is planned by my eye

A boy blocks out the light
in blue shirt and jeans
his long hair over his ears
face young like some pharoah

I am unable to move
with nothing in my hands

We moved in a batch now. Not just Dave Rudabaugh, Wilson and me, but also Garrett, deputies Emory and East, seven others I'd never seen and Charlie lying dead on the horse's back, his arms and legs dangling over the side, tied, so he wouldnt fall off. A sheet covered him to stop him drying too much in the sun. That was a bad week after that. Charlie having taken my hat had got it busted to pieces, so no hat for me as we moved back and forward, side to side over the county, avoiding people and law. Lynchers were out now and, bless him, Garrett didnt want that. So we moved along the Carrizozo plains to the slopes of Oscuros, stayed one night by Chupadero mesa, back to the Carrizozo, passed the Evan tribe, followed now the telegraph to Punta de la Glorietta but over 40 lynchers there. So we moved, no hat for me, uncomfortable times for all of us.

Horses and trains horses and trains. Dave, Wilson and me, our legs handcuffed with long 24″ chains under the horse, our hands bound to the bridle. Five days like that. We had to pee as we sat, into our trousers and down the horse's side. We slept lying forward on the horse's neck. All they did to stop us going mad from saddle pain was alternate saddles, or let us ride bareback one day and a saddle the next. All going grey in the eyes. My horse hating me, the chain under his belly, as much as I hated him.

On the fifth day the sun turned into a pair of hands and began to pull out the hairs in my head. Twist pluck twist pluck. In two hours I was bald, my head like a lemon. It used a fingernail and scratched a knife line from front to back on the skin. A hairline of blood bubbled up and dried. Eleven in the morning then. The sun took a towel and wiped the dried dribble off, like red powder on the towel now. Then with very thin careful fingers it began to unfold my head drawing back each layer of skin and letting it flap over my ears.

The brain juice began to swell up. You could see the bones and grey now. The sun sat back and watched while the juice evaporated. By now the bone was dull white, all dry. When he touched the bone with his fingers it was like brushing raw nerves. He took a thin cold hand and sank it into my head down past the roof of my mouth and washed his fingers in my tongue. Down the long cool hand went scratching the freckles and

76

warts in my throat breaking through veins like pieces of long glass tubing, touched my heart with his wrist, down he went the liquid yellow from my busted brain finally vanishing as it passed through soft warm stomach like a luscious blood wet oasis, weaving in and out of the red yellow blue green nerves moving uncertainly through wrong fissures ending pausing at cul de sacs of bone then retreating slow leaving the pain of suction then down the proper path through pyramids of bone that were there when I was born, through grooves the fingers spanning the merging paths of medians of blue matter, the long cool hand going down brushing cobwebs of nerves the horizontal pain pits, lobules gyres notches arcs tracts fissures roots' white insulation of dead seven year cells clinging things rubbing them off on the tracts of spine down the cool precise fingers went into the cistern of bladder down the last hundred miles in a jerk breaking through my sacs of sperm got my cock in the cool fingers pulled it back up and carried it pulling pulling flabby as smoke up the path his arm had rested in and widened. He brought it up fast half tearing the roots off up the coloured bridges of fibres again, charting the slimy arm back through the pyramids up locked in his fingers up the now bleeding throat up squeezed it through the skull bones, so there I was, my cock standing out of my head. Then he brought his other hand into play I could feel the cool shadow now as he bent over me both his hands tapering into beautiful cool fingers, one hand white as new smelling paper the other 40 colours ochres blues silver from my lung gold and tangerine from the burst ear canals all that clung to him as he went in and came out.

The hands were cold as porcelain, one was silver old bone stripped oak white eastern cigarettes white sky the eye core of sun. Two hands, one dead, one born from me, one like crystal, one like shell of snake found in spring. Burning me like dry ice.

They picked up the fold of foreskin one hand on each side and began the slow pull back back back back *down* like a cap with ear winter muffs like a pair of trousers down boots and then he let go. The wind picked up, I was drowned, locked inside my skin sensitive as an hour old animal, could feel everything, I could hear everything on my skin, as I sat, like a great opaque ostrich egg on the barebacked horse. In my skin hearing

Garrett's voice near me on the skin whats wrong billy whats wrong, couldnt see him but I turned to where I knew he was. I yelled so he could hear me through the skin. Ive been fucked. Ive been fuckd Ive been fucked by Christ almighty god Ive been good and fucked by Christ. And I rolled off the horse's back like a soft shell-less egg wrapped in thin white silk and I splashed onto the dust blind and white but the chain held my legs to the horse and I was dragged picking up dust on my wet skin as I travelled in between his four trotting legs at last thank the fucking christ, in the shade of his stomach.

Garrett moved us straight to the nearest railroad depot. We had to wait one night for the train that would take us to Messilla where they would hold the trial. The Polk Hotel there was a bright white place with a wide courtyard and well. The deputies went down in the bucket and washed themselves. They removed Charlie off his horse. Garrett took over and washed the dried blood off the animal. Garrett ordered a box for Charlie Bowdre. Then he made me drink liquids and paste. They had to carry the three of us from the horses to the beds — we couldn't walk after the week on horses. I was to share a room with Garrett and Emory.

Your last good bed Billy, he said, pick your position. I did, face and stomach down. He chained me to the bed. He taped my fingers so thick I couldnt get them through a trigger guard even if they gave me a gun. Then he went out and looked after Wilson who had broken both ankles when the horse stumbled collapsing on his chained legs.

It is afternoon still, the room white with light. My last white room, the sun coming through the shutters making the white walls whiter. I lie on my left cheek looking to that light. I cannot even see the door or if Emory has stayed behind. The bed vast. Went to sleep, my body melting into it. I remember once after Charlie and I stopped talking we could hear flies buzzing in their black across a room, and I remember once, one night in the open I turned to say goodnight to Charlie who was about ten yards away and there was the moon balanced perfect on his nose.

It is the order of the court that you
be taken to Lincoln and confined to
jail until May 13th and that on that
day between the hours of sunrise and
noon you be hanged on the gallows
until you are dead dead dead
And may God have mercy on your
soul

said Judge Warren H. Bristol

THE KID TELLS ALL

'EXCLUSIVE JAIL INTERVIEW'

INTERVIEWER: Billy...

BONNEY: Mr. Bonney please.

I: Mr. Bonney, I am from the *Texas Star*. You are now how old?

B: 21.

I: When is your birthday?

B: November 23rd. On that lap I'll be 22.

I: You were reported as saying, as adding, to that phrase — 'If I make it' when asked that question before.

B: Well, sometimes I feel more confident than at others.

I: And you feel alright now...

B: Yes, I'm ok now.

I: Mr. Bonney, when you rejected Governor Houston's offer of an amnesty, were you aware of the possibility that your life would continue the way it has?

B: Well, I don't know; Charlie, Charlie Bowdre that is, said then that I was a fool not to grab what I could out of old Houston. But what the hell. It didn't mean too much then anyway. All Houston was offering me was protection from the law, and at that time the law had no quarrels with me, so it seemed rather silly.

I: But you were wanted for cattle rustling weren't you?

B: Yes, but, well let me put it this way. I could only be arrested if they had proof, definite proof, not just stories. They had to practically catch me with stolen cattle in my bed. And when you rustle, you can see law coming a good two miles away. All I had to do was ride off in the opposite direction and that would have been that.

I: But couldn't they catch you with them when you sold them?

B: Well I don't do, I didn't do the selling — I sold them off before they reached the market.

I: How were, or with whom were you able to do that?

B: I'd rather not mention names if you don't mind.

(Here Mr. Bonney withdrew a black cigarette, lit it, and grinned charmingly, then retreated behind his enigmatic half smile, a smile which was on the verge of one. These smiles of 'Billy the Kid' are well known and have become legendary among his friends in this area. Sherriff Garrett has an explanation for this:

"Billy has a denture system which is prominent, buck teeth you at the paper would call it. So that even when he has no intention of smiling his teeth force his mouth into a half grin. Because of this, people are always amazed at his high spirits in a time of stress." Mrs. Celsa Guitterrez adds to this:

"When Billy was 18, a man named John Rapsey ('. . . . head' as he was affectionately called afterwards) broke his (Billy's) nose with a bottle. Billy was knocked unconscious and Rapsey escaped. Bowdre who was with him, to ease the pain when he came to, fed him some tequila, made him drunk. Billy didn't get his nose fixed for three days as Bowdre accompanying him on the tequila also got drunk and forgot all about the broken nose. As a result, when Billy finally got to Sumner to get it fixed his breathing channels, or whatever, were clogged. After that he rarely breathed through his nose again, and breathed by sucking the air in through his mouth, or through his teeth as it seemed. If you were near him when he was breathing heavily — when excited or running, you could hear this hissing noise which was quite loud.")

B: Anyway, Houston offered me protection from the law, and the only law I knew in Fort Sumner was the Murphy faction which would certainly not uphold Houston if they found me in a dark street without guns. (Laugh)

I: Did you get on well with Houston?

B: He was ok.

I: What do you mean by that?

B: Just that he was straight about it all. I mean he was disappointed of course that I couldn't agree, but I think he saw my point. I don't think he thought much of Murphy's men, or trusted them either.

I: But right now you've threatened to kill him if you escape this hanging?

B: WHEN I escape, yes.

I: Why?

B: Well, I've been through all this before. I've already made a statement. But anyway, again. In my trial three weeks ago, the charge that was brought against me was for shooting Sherriff Clark, etc. Now Houston offered me parole, or amnesty or whatever *after* this shooting. As you know there were no real witnesses of any murder on my part after that incident. But the fact is that the Clark shooting took place during the Lincoln County war — when EVERYBODY was shooting. I mean no one brought charges against those who shot McSween or Tunstall. Now Houston when he spoke to me admitted that, while he couldn't condone what was done during those three days, he understood that both sides were guilty, and like a state of war there was no criminal punishment that could be genuinely brought against me without bringing it against everyone connected with that war. Two wrongs make a right, right? Now they find that because they cannot charge me with anything else that'll stick they charge me for something that happened during a war . A fact that your Governor Houston realises and I'm sure privately admits and still won't do anything about.

I: Why do you suppose he doesn't do anything to pardon you now?

B: (Giggling) Well I suppose he's been wished into thinking that I've been pretty nasty since. But the point is that there is no legal proof to all this later stuff. The evidence used was unconstitutional.

I: Do you have a lawyer, I mean working on an appeal now?

B: Slip me a gun and I will have — don't print that.

I: Mr. Bonney, or may I call you Billy. . .

B: No.

I: Mr. Bonney, do you believe in God?

B: No.

I: Why not, and for how long haven't you?

B: Well I did for a long time, I mean in a superstitious way, same way I believe in luck for instance. I couldn't take the risk you see. Like never wearing anything yellow. So before big fights, or even the most minor as well as the really easy ones, I used to cross myself and say, "God please don't let me die today." I did this fast though so no one would see me, see what I was doing. I did this pretty well every day from the age of 12 till I was 18. When I was 18, I had a shooting match with Tom O'Folliard, the prize was a horse. Now it was with rifles and Tom is excellent with them and I wanted that horse very much. I prayed every day. Then I lost the bet with Tom.

I: Do you worry about what will happen after death now you don't believe in God?

B: Well I try to avoid it. Though I suppose not. I guess they'll just put you in a box and you will stay there forever. There'll be nothing else. The only thing I wish is that I could hear what people say afterwards. I'd really like that. You know, I'd like to be invisible watching what happens to people when I am not around. I suppose you thing that's simple minded.

I: Are you happy, or at least were you happy? Did you have any reason for going on living, or were you just experimenting?

B: I don't know whether I'm happy or not. But in the end that is all that's important — that you keep testing yourself, as you say — experimenting on how good you are, and you can't do that when you want to lose.

I: Is that all you looked forward to?

B: Yes I suppose so. And my friends. I enjoy people and being with friends.

I: Is it true that you were going to get married and move east when you were arrested?

B: As I say I don't want to cause trouble, and though I'm not saying about the first part of the question, I *had* intended to leave the area cos people kept coming up to me and saying I was going to get it for what I had done to their friends. Bob Ollinger who's worked his way into being my jailer. He had a close friend who was killed in the Lincoln County war.

I: Who do you consider your friends now, now that Bowdre and O'Folliard are dead?

B: Well I have some. Dave Rudabaugh wherever he is. I guess he's locked up too somewhere. They won't tell me. A couple of guys here and there. A couple of ladies.

I: Garrett?

B: Well Pat's right now a . . . . head. We used to be friends as you probably know. He's got senile. He's getting a lot of money for cleaning the area up — of us supposedly. No I don't think much of him now.   .

I: He's said that he gave you all plenty of opportunity to get out of New Mexico before he began hunting you.

B: Yeahhhh but one) you don't go around using mutual friends to trap an old friend and two) I love the country around here and Fort Sumner. . .all my friends are here. I'd go now, cos some I thought were friends were really pretty hypocritical.

I: What about pastimes? Did you have many when you were free? Did you like books, music, dancing?

B: Dancing I like, I'm a pretty good dancer. Fond of music too. There's a Canadian group, a sort of orchestra, that is the best. Great. Heard them often when I was up there trying to get hold of a man who went by the name of Captain P————.* Never found him. But that group will be remembered a long time.

I: How about you, do you think you will last in people's memories?

B: I'll be with the world till she dies.

I: But what do you think you'll be remembered as? I mean don't you think that already several feel you are morally vulgar? I mean all these editorials about you. . . .

B: Well. . .editorials. A friend of Garrett's, Mr. Cassavates or something, said something bout editorials. He said editorials don't do anything they just make people feel guilty.

I: That's rather good.

B: Yes. It is.

Am the dartboard
for your midnight blood
the bones' moment
of perfect movement
that waits to be thrown
magnetic into combat

a pencil
harnessing my face
goes stumbling into dots

No the escape was no surprise to me. I expected it. I really did, we all did I suppose. And it is now in retrospect difficult to describe. You've probably read the picture books anyway, seen the films, of how he did it. What he did was to seduce young Bell into a cardgame, shot him, then shot Ollinger returning from lunch. Nobody cared about Ollinger, but Bell was liked. You know how Ollinger used to kill people? He'd go up to them about to shake hands, then grab their right hand with his left, lift out his pistol and fire into the chest. He had hated Billy ever since the Lincoln County War. So Bell and Ollinger died and Billy escaped. Also on the way out of town he hit a man named Ellery Fleck in the face, with his rifle, for no reason at all. He was probably elated.

One funny thing happened apparently (I was out of town). Billy's hands were still chained, and jumping onto a horse to escape he lost his balance and fell off — right in front of the crowd who refused to do anything but watch. In that crowd nobody cracked a smile. Three or four kids helped him catch the horse and held it while he got on carefully. Then with the rifle cradled in his arms he made the horse walk slowly over Ollinger's body and went.

MISS SALLIE CHISUM :

GOOD FRIENDS :

As far as dress was concerned
he always looked as if
he had just stepped out of a bandbox.

In broadbrimmed white hat
dark coat and vest
grey trousers worn over his boots
a grey flannel shirt
and black four-in-hand tie
and sometimes — would you believe it ? —
a flower in his lapel.

A COURTEOUS LITTLE GENTLEMAN:

I suppose it sounds absurd to speak
of such a character as a gentleman,
but from beginning to end
of our long relationship,
in all his personal relations with me,
he was the pink of politeness
and as courteous a little gentleman
as I ever met.

There was a brook full of fish
that ran under the house
across a corner of the kitchen
and I often sat on the back porch
in a rocking chair, with Billy
to bait my hook for me,
and caught a string of perch for dinner.

(Garrett had stuffed birds. Not just the stringy Mexican vultures but huge exotic things. We would sometimes be with him when they arrived. He would have them sent to him frozen in boxes. The box was wooden, a crate really, and with great care after bringing it back from the station, he would remove the nails. He first took out the 8″ of small crushed ice and said look. And it would be a white seagull. It was beautifully spread in the ice, not a feather out of place, its claws extended and brittle from the freezing. Garrett melted it and split it with a narrow knife, parting the feathers first, and with a rubber glove in his right hand removed the body. He then washed the rotted blood from the wings, the outside, and then took it out onto the verandah to dry.)

MISS SALLIE CHISUM : PAT GARRETT

A tremendously tall man.

Despite his crooked mouth
and crooked smile which
made his whole face seem crooked

he was a remarkably handsome man.

BILLY THE KID & PAT GARRETT ; SOME FINAL THOUGHTS :

I knew both these men intimately.
There was good mixed in with the bad
in Billy the Kid
and bad mixed in with the good
in Pat Garrett.

No matter what they did in the world
or what the world thought of them
they were my friends.
Both were worth knowing.

Sound up. Loud and vibrating in the room. My ears picking up all the burning hum of flies letting go across the room. The mattress under Pete Maxwell shifting its straw, each blade loud in its clear flick against another. Even the now and then crack at the glass as the day's heat evaporates from the window against the dark of the desert.

And then that breathing, not Maxwell's but *the other's.* The breathing precise but forced into quiet but regular streams. Think of the dark air going up through the nose, down to the stomach rolling around on itself, and then up and out like a fountain spilling through his teeth hissssssssssss ssssssssssssssss

MMMmmmmmmm. In the final minutes. It is Texas midnight. A large large square, well and buckets centre. The houses and sheds in rows making up the square. The long narrow porch running all around. Up to the well rides Pat Garrett and deputies Poe and Mackinnon. Scuffling slow, smoking as they dismount gentle and leave the horses and walk to the large hut which is Maxwell's room. They pass the dog.

This is a diagram then of Maxwell's, Pete Maxwell's, room. Bed here against the wall, here's the window where he put his hand through. And here, along here, is the porch. While this, about 20 yards away, is the Guitterrez home. Garrett, Poe, and Mackinnon stop near Maxwell's door. On some vague tip Garrett has come to ask Maxwell where he thinks Billy is hiding out — where in the territory is he — he's been escaped 3 months and nobody's seen him. Garrett leaves the deputies sitting smoking on the porch, flicks away his own cigar and goes into the dark room where Maxwell is asleep *Meanwhile*

Billy is just yards away drinking with Celsa Guitterrez. He came in about an hour ago, he wears only his trousers and guns, hot night. They decide she will cook him something and he offers to go cut some meat. Carrying a knife in his left hand, and barefoot, he is up and begins walking towards the ice house. Passing the Maxwell room he sees the two men outside. Quien es? They do not answer. Again the question. No answer. Billy backs off the porch into Maxwell's room and heads towards his friend's sleeping.

In the dark room Garrett has wakened and is questioning the dazed Maxwell. In fact as Billy enters he is crouching by Maxwell's bed. Quienes son esos hombres afuera, Pete? Garrett recognises the voice. He does the one thing that will save him. Quietly, with his long legs, he climbs over Maxwell's body and gets into bed between Maxwell and the wall. With his rifle in his hands he watches the darkness, trying to make out the shape that is moving towards him. Billy moves over barefoot and asks Pete again. Quienes son esos hombres afuera?

Maxwell doesn't say a word. He can feel Garrett's oiled rifle barrel leaning against his cheek. Billy shakes Maxwell's shoulder and then he hears the other person's breathing. As the only other woman on the ranch, apart from Celsa Guitterrez is Paulita Maxwell — Pete's sister — he doesn't know what to think. Paulita? Pete Maxwell gives a nervous giggle full of fear which Billy mistakes for embarrassment. Paulita! Jesus Christ. He leans forward again and moves his hands down the bed and then feels a man's boots. O my god Pete quien es?

He is beginning to move back a couple of yards in amazement. Garrett is about to burst out laughing so he fires, leaving a powder scar on Maxwell's face that stayed with him all his life.

OUTSIDE
  the outline of houses
  Garrett running from a door
  — all seen sliding round
  the screen of a horse's eye

NOW dead centre in the square is Garrett with Poe
— hands in back pockets — argues, nodding his head
and then ALL TURNING as the naked arm, the arm from
the body, breaks through the window. The window —
what remains between the splits — reflecting all the
moving too.

Guitterrez goes to hold the arm but it is manic, breaks
her second finger. His veins that controlled triggers —
now tearing all they touch.

The end of it, lying at the wall
the bullet itch frozen in my head

my right arm is through the window pane
and the cut veins awake me
so I can watch inside and through the window

Garrett's voice going Billy Billy
and the other two dancing circles
saying we got him we got him the little shrunk bugger

the pain at my armpit I'm glad for
keeping me alive at the bone
and suns coming up everywhere out of the walls and floors
Garrett's jaw and stomach   thousands

of lovely perfect sun balls
breaking at each other click
click click click like Saturday morning pistol cleaning
when the bullets hop across the bed sheet and bounce and click

click and you toss them across the floor like . . . up in the air
and see how many you can catch in one hand the left

oranges reeling across the room AND I KNOW I KNOW
it is my brain coming out like red grass
this breaking where red things wade

PAULITA MAXWELL .

*An old story that identifies me as Billy the Kid's
sweetheart has been going the rounds for many years.
Perhaps it honours me; perhaps not; it depends on how
you feel about it. But I was not Billy the Kid's sweetheart
I liked him very much — oh, yes — but I did not love
him. He was a nice boy, at least to me, courteous, gallant,
always respectful. I used to meet him at dances; he was
of course often at our home. But he and I had not
thought of marriage.*

*There was a story that Billy and I had laid our plans to
elope to old Mexico and had fixed the date for the night
just after that on which he was killed. There was another
tale that we proposed to elope riding double on one
horse. Neither story was true and the one about eloping
on one horse was a joke. Pete Maxwell, my brother, had
more horses than he knew what to do with, and if Billy
and I had wanted to set off for the Rio Grande by the
light of the moon, you may depend upon it we would at
least have had separate mounts. I did not need to put my
arms around any man's waist to keep from falling off a
horse. Not I. I was, if you please, brought up in the
saddle, and plumed myself on my horsemanship.*

Imagine if you dug him up and brought him out. You'd see very little. There'd be the buck teeth. Perhaps Garrett's bullet no longer in thick wet flesh would roll in the skull like a marble. From the head there'd be a trail of vertebrae like a row of pearl buttons off a rich coat down to the pelvis. The arms would be cramped on the edge of what was the box. And a pair of handcuffs holding ridiculously the fine ankle bones. (Even though dead they buried him in leg irons). There would be the silver from the toe of each boot.

His legend a jungle sleep

Billy the Kid and the Princess

The Castel of the Spanish girl called 'La Princesa' towered above the broad fertile valley . . . in the looming hills there were gold and silver mines . . . Truly, the man chosen to rule beside the loveliest woman in Mexico would be a king. The girl had chosen William H. Bonney to reign with her . . . but a massive brute named Toro Cuneo craved that honor. . .

There'd been a cattle war in Jackson County . . . He'd settled a beef with three gunquick brothers near Tucson. . . and he was weary of gunthunder and sudden death! Billy the Kid turned his cayuse south . . . splashed across the drought dried Rio Grande . . . and let the sun bake the tension out of his mind and body.

"See them sawtooth peaks, Caballo? There's a little town yonder with a real cold cerveza and a fat lady who can cook Mexican food better'n anybody in the world! This lady also got a daughter . . . una muchacho . . . who's got shinin' black hair and a gleam in her brown eyes I want to see again."

And on a distant hill . . .
"He comes, be ready Soto."

"Gunshots . . . a 45 pistol! Runaway! It's a girl! She's goin' to take a spill! Faster Chico!"
"AAAAAHH!"
"Hang on . . . I got yuh! . . . You're okay now Señorita."
"Gracias, Señor. You are so strong and brave . . . and very gallant!"

"Thanks, I heard shots . . . Did they scare your cayuse into runnin' away?"

"I think I can stand now, Señor . . . if you will put me down."

"Huh? Oh sorry, Señorita. I'm Billy Bonney, Señorita. I'm from up around Tucson."

"I am Marguerita Juliana de Guelva y Solanza, la Princesa de Guelva."

"La Princesa? A *real* princess?"

"I am direct descendent of King Phillip of Spain. By virtue of Royal land grants, I own this land west for 200 leagues, south for 180 leagues. It is as large as some European kingdoms . . . larger than two of your American states . . . I am still a little weak. Ride with me to the castle, Señor Bonney."

"*There* Señor Bonney . . . my ancestral home. The castle and the valley farther than you can see . . . I have 20,000 cattle, almost as many horses and herds of goats, pigs, chickens. Everything my people need to live."

"WHOOOEEE! The Governor's mansion up at Phoenix would fit in one end o' that wickiup."

"Come on, Yanqui! It is late . . . you must have dinner with me."

"ATTENTION! HER EXCELLENCY RETURNS!"
Thinks: "She's got a regular army!"

The man called Billy the Kid is not impressed by the magnificent richness of his surroundings. The golden cutlery means nothing . . . The priceless china and crystal matter not, and the food cooked by a French chef? — PFAAGGH!
Thinks: "I'd sooner be in Mama Rosa's kitchen eatin' tortillas an' chile with Rosita battin' them dark eyes at me!"

"This table needs a man like you, Señor Bonney. Others have occupied that chair but none so well as you."

"Gracias, Princesa . . . but I'd never feel right in it . . . if you know what I mean."

"I propose a toast, my gringo friend . . . to our meeting . . . to your gallant rescue of me!"

"I reckon I can't let a lady drink alone, Princesa."

CRASH! ! !

"He could have sunk it in my neck just as easy . . . Start talkin' hombre 'fore I say *my* piece about that knife throwing act!"

"I am a man of action, not words, gringo! I weel crack your ribs . . . break your wrists . . . then send you back where you belong!"

"Come on, animal, I want to finish dinner!"

SOCK! !

Thinks: "If I can nail him quick I'll take the fight out of him . . . PERFECT!"

That was his Sunday punch . . . and Toro laughed at it! Now, Billy the Kid knows he's in for a struggle!

"He's got a granite jaw which means . . . I'll have to weaken him with powerful hooks to the stomach! OOOOWWW!" THUD!

"Now it's my turn!"

"If he lays a hand on me . . ."

SWISSS!

SOCK!

"I keel you gringo!"

Thinks: "My head . . . he busted my jaw!"

TOCK!

Thinks: "He's a stomper . . ."

"I keel your pet gringo Excellencia!"

"Yuh'll take me tuh death maybe, hombre!"

"You no escape Toro now!"

"I didn't figure on escapin' Toro!"

CRACK!

"Over you go, Toro!" "Olé! Olé!"

CRASH!

"Sorry I busted the place up some, Princesa."

"You are mucho hombre, Yanqui, very much man! A man like you could help me rule this wild kingdom! Will you remain as my guest for a time?"

"I come down here to rest up some. I reckon I can do that here as well as in Mama Rosa's cantina."

(Kiss)

"That was to thank you for protecting me from Toro Cueno. I must not go on being formal with you . . ."

In the next few days, Billy the Kid was with La Princesa often. Long rides through wild country . . .

"Wait princess . . . don't get ahead of me!"

"EEEEEeeii! !"

"Duck, princess!"

BANG! BANG!

"Once more Chivoto, you have saved my life, this time from that cougar. You have won my love!"

"Hold on, ma'am . . ."

Before Billy the Kid can defend himself, La Princesa Marguerita has taken him in her arms and . . . .

"It was the Kid who came in there on to me," Garrett told Poe,
"and I think I got him."

"Pat," replied Poe, "I believe you have killed the wrong man."

"I'm sure it was the Kid," responded Garrett, "for I knew his
voice and could not have been mistaken."

Poor young William's dead
with a fish stare, with a giggle
with blood planets in his head.

The blood came down like river ride
long as Texas down his side.
We cleaned him up when blood was drier
his eyes looked up like turf on fire.

We got the eight foot garden hose
turned it on, leaned him down flat.
What fell away we threw away
his head was smaller than a rat.

I got the bullets, cleaned him up
sold them to the Texas Star.
They weighed them, put them in a pile
took pictures with a camera.

Poor young William's dead
with blood planets in his head
with a fish stare, with a giggle
like he said.

It is now early morning, was a bad night. The hotel room seems large. The morning sun has concentrated all the cigarette smoke so one can see it hanging in pillars or sliding along the roof like amoeba. In the bathroom, I wash the loose nicotene out of my mouth. I smell the smoke still in my shirt.

This book is for many but especially for Kim, Stuart and Sally Mackinnon, Ken Livingstone, Victor Coleman and Barrie Nichol.

ACKNOWLEDGMENTS:
Some sections of *The Collected Works* have appeared in magazines so I would like to thank the magazines and their editors. Blew Ointment, Is, 20 Cents Magazine, Quarry. And the following books: *The Cosmic Chef* and *The Story So Far.*

Published with the assistance of the Canada Council

First Printing 1970

ISBN: 0 88784 018 3 (paper);
0 88784 118 X (cloth).

Library of Congress Card Number: 74-132927.

Michael Ondaatje's other books include *The Dainty Monsters* (Coach House 1967) and *The Man with Seven Toes* (Coach House 1969). He has also made a documentary film called *Sons of Captain Poetry* (1970). He has two children and is married to the painter Kim Ondaatje. He teaches at Glendon College, Toronto. *The Collected Works of Billy the Kid* was written while he lived in London Ontario 1967-70.

CREDITS:

The death of Tunstall, the reminiscences by Paulita Maxwell
and Sallie Chisum on Billy, are essentially made up of statements
made to Walter Noble Burns in his book *The Saga of Billy the
Kid* published in 1926. The comment about taking photographs
around 1870-80 is by the great Western photographer L.A.
Huffman and appears in his book *Huffman, Frontier Photographer.* (Some of the photographs in this book are his.) The
last piece of dialogue between Garrett and Poe is taken from an
account written by Deputy John W. Poe in 1919 when he was
the President of the National Bank of Roswell, New Mexico.
The comic book legend, *Billy the Kid and the Princess,* is   Inc.
© 1969 Carlton Press, Inc., by permission.
With these basic sources I have edited, rephrased, and slightly
reworked the originals. But the emotions belong to their authors.

The cover is by Roger Silvester.

Designed at The Coach House Press, September 1970

Published by the House of Anansi Press
35 Britain Street, Toronto, Canada

6   7   8   9   10   11   78